This edition published by
Coles, Canada
by arrangement with Twin Books

© 1992 Twin Books UK Ltd

Produced by
TWIN BOOKS
Kimbolton House
117A Fulham Road
London SW3 6RL
England

Directed by CND – Muriel Nathan-Deiller
Illustrated by Van Gool-Lefèvre-Loiseaux
Adapted from the play "Peter Pan" by J.M. Barrie
Text adapted by Barbara Paulding Thrasher

ISBN: 1-85469-952-0

Printed in Hong Kong

"'VAN GOOL'S'"

Peter Pan

It was a dark night in London, and Mr and Mrs Darling, helped by Nana the dog, were putting their children to bed.

"Come on, you lot, it's time to go to bed," said Mrs Darling.

"Look Mummy, Peter Pan has been flying in here!" shouted Wendy, the eldest. "Here are some leaves from his suit. Peter, where are you?"

"In Never-Never Land!" shouted John and Michael.

"What nonsense you're babbling!" said Mr Darling. "Sleep well, and don't dream about Peter Pan, he doesn't exist."

Later that evening Mrs Darling was sitting near the children's room sewing. It was so quiet she had fallen asleep, but she was awoken suddenly by the rustle of leaves. She opened her eyes and let out a cry: there was a boy flying around the room!

Nana was sitting with her, and chased the flying boy out the window. But, before he could escape, Nana caught hold of Peter Pan's shadow.

The next day before breakfast, Michael refused to take his medicine. "Do be reasonable, Michael!" said Mr Darling "Do it like this." He lifted a glass to his lips.

But Mr Darling did not drink the
medicine. By sleight of hand he poured
it into Nana's bowl instead. Poor Nana
– she drank the medicine and fell
straight asleep! And she was supposed
to look after the children that night,
because Mr and Mrs Darling were
going out to a party!

Later that night, Peter Pan flew by
the Darling household. All the lights
were out, but he was preceded by a
flickering light. He went up to the
nursery window which, as it was
summer, was open during the night.
He had come to get his shadow back
which Nana had seized the night
before.

Peter found his shadow lurking in the nursery, but it didn't want to go back with him.

"Come here, you stubborn shadow!" cried Peter, who was getting very angry.

Just then Wendy woke up,
because of all the noise Peter
was making.
    "Oh Peter, you're back!
Come here with your shadow,
and I'll sew it on for you."

When she was finished
Peter gave Wendy a necklace
by way of a thank you
present.
    "Peter, it's lovely!"
exclaimed Wendy. Then she
saw the flickering light that
had arrived with Peter.
"You've not come on your
own this time?"
    "Wendy, this is Tinker
Bell."

"I've an idea!" said Peter. "Why don't you come back to Never-Never Land with us?"

Wendy woke up John and Michael. "We're going to Never-Never Land with Peter! Come on!"

Tinker Bell sprinkled them all with glittering pixie dust and the children rose into the air. They flew out the nursery window over the rooftops of London.

After flying for a long time, the small group arrived at
Never-Never Land. "Go on Tinker, you lead the way.
It's so dark . . ." said Peter. Suddenly—WHIZZZ! A red
light flashed across the sky.

"A cannonball! Watch out Wendy, the pirates are
firing at us." But the warning came too late, and they
were separated. . . .

Meanwhile, Captain Hook, the leader of the pirates, had left his ship and had just stepped ashore.

"You idiots!" he cried. "You missed Peter Pan! We must find the hideaway of the Lost Boys and capture them. When my hand was cut off by Peter and given to the crocodile, I vowed to get revenge, and you're not helping me!"

"Captain, please don't shout like that. The crocodile will hear you, and if his clock has stopped we'll not hear him approach."

The pirates started to look around
for signs of the Lost Boys.
"Strange . . . This mushroom looks
like a chimney! I can hear the voices
. . . I will find them! My vengeance will
be terrible!" exclaimed Hook.

But suddenly Captain Hook's face went white. He heard a *tick-tock, tick-tock, tick-tock*.

"The croc. . . the croco. . . the crocodile! Help!" yelled Hook, and he raced back towards the boat. He promised they would be back, though. He had heard the Lost Boys say that they were waiting for Peter Pan to return.

Wendy was lost in the sky above
Never-Never Land with Tinker Bell.

"I will leave her," thought Tinker
Bell. "She wants to take Peter away
from me!" And with that she flew
straight to the Lost Boys.

"What's that, Tinker? Peter wants us
to shoot down a great white bird?"
Keen to obey Peter's wishes, the Lost
Boys picked up their slingshots and
bows and arrows.

Struck by one of the rocks, Wendy fell to the ground.

"What have you done?" asked Peter as he arrived back. "I was bringing you a mother to tell you stories, and you've killed her!"

"But Peter, Tinker Bell said that you wanted us to knock her out of the sky," protested one of the Lost Boys.

"Tinker Bell, how could you? Go away! I don't want to see you again!"

Just then Wendy moved an arm, and slowly sat up.

"She's alive!" whispered the Lost Boys in unison.

"I'm OK," said Wendy. There was a shuffling behind her. John and Michael had appeared, too.

Two new friends and a mother! The Lost Boys were very happy, and took everyone back to their hideaway.

From then on, Wendy took charge of the Lost Boys in their underground home. They all ate well, went to bed early, and Wendy told them lots of stories. Tinker Bell, hiding in a nest high up in the wall out of sight, listened to the stories too. She was extremely jealous of Wendy.

During the day, Peter showed Wendy and her brothers the island sights. He took them to meet the mermaids, who took a strong dislike to Wendy as soon as they saw her.

"Send her away, Peter, then we can play," they called out rudely.

Wendy was a little upset at being disliked so much before she had even had a chance to speak!

Suddenly Peter hissed, "Look!" Then he whispered to Wendy and the others, "Pirates! They've captured the Indian Chief's daughter, Tiger Lily. Quick – we must help!"

"They are going to tie her to that rock and she'll drown at high tide!" exclaimed Wendy.

Hiding behind a rock, Peter imitated Captain Hook's voice. "Get out," he said. "Release Tiger Lily."

"But Captain," protested the pirates, "you said . . ."

"I've changed my plans. Just do as you're told!" The two pirates let Tiger Lily go, and she dived into the water and swam for the shore.

The real Captain Hook arrived at that moment.
"Where is Tiger Lily?" he demanded.
"Hello, Hook!" said Peter Pan, appearing before him.
"I've let Tiger Lily go!"
Hook, furious that yet another of his dastardly plans
had gone wrong because of Peter Pan, drew his sword
and a terrible fight ensued.

Chasing after Hook on the rocks, Peter slipped and fell. Captain Hook bashed him on the head with his hook, then returned to his ship, thinking that Peter would be drowned when high tide came along. "Revenge at last," he thought.

But Wendy, who had been watching everything from behind a rock, came to Peter's rescue. "How are we going to get home?" she wondered out loud. "You're too feeble to fly and I'm not strong enough to support you."

They stayed there for some time, while Peter slept.
The water was slowly rising up the rock.

"Look, Peter!" shouted Wendy suddenly. "There's
Michael's kite. I'm sure that could help us to get back."
Reaching out, she caught hold of the string, and they
gently floated away from the rock.

Wendy and Peter arrived back safely. While Peter rested, Wendy told the Lost Boys another story. She was missing her parents, so she told the Lost Boys all about them.

"Why don't you come back to London with us?" she suggested, "I'm sure our parents will adopt you." There was a general chorus of approval from the Lost Boys.

"I want to stay here," said Peter sadly. "I don't want to grow up."

Ever since Tiger Lily had been saved from the pirates by Peter Pan, the Indians had mounted a watch outside the Lost Boys' home to protect them. However, the pirates still managed to attack and tie up all the Indian guards in the middle of the night.

In the morning one of the pirates played the tom-tom. Hearing the drum signal, the children thought it was safe to leave their home.

47

Not suspecting anything to be wrong, the Lost Boys, Wendy, John and Michael filed out of the hideaway ready to fly to the Darling home.

"Tie them up!" shouted Captain Hook.

"Peter! Help us!" cried Michael.

"What's this? Peter Pan is *alive*!" sputtered the angry Captain. "Take the prisoners to the ship. This time I'm going to really finish him off."

He crept into the underground
house, and the sleeping Peter didn't
hear him. Hook placed a bottle of
poison, marked "Peter," on a table
near his bed, then left quietly.

Tinker Bell saw everything, of course. As soon as Hook had left she flew out from her hiding place in the wall and pushed the bottle off the table. It crashed onto the floor. The noise woke Peter.

"What's happening?" he asked her.

So Tinker Bell told Peter about the ambush of Wendy and the boys by the pirates, and about Hook's plan to poison him.

On board the pirate ship John and Michael were walking down the plank very bravely. Wendy, tied to the main mast, shouted her goodbyes to her brothers. Just then a sound could be heard approaching the side of the ship, *Tick-tock, tick-tock, tick-tock*. Hook went green with fear . . . the crocodile was back! The boys came to a halt at the end of the plank.

At the same time Peter sprang up from behind the crocodile and landed on the plank. He cut the ropes that were tied around Michael and John, then released Wendy. The pirates surrounded their captain, who was about to faint. The crocodile was still waiting for his dinner.

The children fought the pirates in a fierce battle. It was not long before the pirates (who hadn't had a proper fight in ages) began to get tired.

Wendy and her brothers chased the pirates around the ship until, in a bid to escape them, they all jumped into the sea.

Peter was still fighting with Hook, who suddenly lost his balance and went tumbling into the sea, where the crocodile waited for him.

After their spectacular victory, Wendy announced that she still wanted to go back home. Peter agreed to show them the way.

"The Lost Boys can stay with you if they want, but I'm going to come back here to Never-Never Land." declared Peter.

And what a surprise for Mr and Mrs Darling when they saw their children again, with all those new friends.

The Darlings agreed to let
the Lost Boys stay.

"And Peter?" whispered
Wendy, watching him fly
away.

"I'll come back for you
once a year, Wendy," cried
Peter, "for holidays in Never-
Never Land."